HELLO, I'M THEA!

I'm *Geronimo Stilton*'s sister. As I'm sure you know from my brother's bestselling novels, I'm a special correspondent for *The Rodent's Gazette*, Mouse Island's most famouse newspaper. Unlike my 'fraidy mouse brother, I absolutely adore traveling, having adventures, and meeting rodents from all around the world!

The adventure I want to tell you about begins at Mouseford Academy, the school I went to when I was a young mouseling. I had such a great experience there as a student that I came back to teach a journalism class.

When I returned as a grown mouse, I met five really special students: Colette, Nicky, Pamela, Paulina, and Violet. You could hardly imagine five more different mouselings, but they became great friends right away. And they liked me so much that they decided to name their group after me: the Thea Sisters! I was so touched by that, I decided to write about their adventures. So turn the page to read a fabumouse adventure about the

THEA SISTERS!

Name: Nicky

Nickname: Nic

Home: Australia

Secret ambition: Wants to be an ecologist.

Loves: Open spaces and nature.

Strengths: She is always in a good mood, as long as she's outdoors!

Weaknesses: She can't sit still!

Secret: Nicky is claustrophobic—she can't stand being in small, tight places.

Nicky

COLETTE

Name: Colette

Nickname: It's Colette, please. (She can't stand nicknames.)

Home: France

Secret ambition: Colette is very particular about her appearance. She wants to be a fashion writer.

Loves: The color pink.

Strengths: She's energetic and full of great ideas.

Weaknesses: She's always late!

Secret: To relax, there's nothing Colette likes more than a manicure and pedicure.

Colette

VIOLET

Name: Violet
Nickname: Vi
Home: China
Secret ambition: Wants to become a great violinist.
Loves: Books! She is a real intellectual, just like my brother, Geronimo.
Strengths: She's detail-oriented and always open to new things.
Weaknesses: She is a bit sensitive and can't stand being teased. And if she doesn't get enough sleep, she can be a real grouch!
Secret: She likes to unwind by listening to classical music and drinking green tea.

Violet

Name: Paulina
Nickname: Polly
Home: Peru
Secret ambition: Wants to be a scientist.
Loves: Traveling and meeting people from all over the world. She is also very close to her sister, Maria.
Strengths: Loves helping other rodents.
Weaknesses: She's shy and can be a bit clumsy.
Secret: She is a computer genius!

PAULINA

PAULINA

Name: Pamela
Nickname: Pam
Home: Tanzania

Secret ambition: Wants to become a sports journalist or a car mechanic.

Loves: Pizza, pizza, and more pizza! She'd eat pizza for breakfast if she could.

Strengths: She is a peacemaker. She can't stand arguments.

Weaknesses: She is very impulsive.

Secret: Give her a screwdriver and any mechanical problem will be solved!

Pamela

Geronimo Stilton

Thea Stilton
AND THE MYSTERY ON
THE ORIENT EXPRESS

Scholastic Inc.

No part of this publication may be reproduced, stored in a retrieval system, or transmitted in any form or by any means, electronic, mechanical, photocopying, recording, or otherwise, without written permission from the copyright holder. For information regarding permission, please contact: Atlantyca S.p.A., Via Leopardi 8, 20123 Milan, Italy; e-mail foreignrights@atlantyca.it, www.atlantyca.com.

ISBN 978-0-545-34105-9

Copyright © 2010 by Edizioni Piemme S.p.A., Corso Como 15, 20154 Milan, Italy.

International Rights © Atlantyca S.p.A.

English translation © 2012 by Atlantyca S.p.A.

GERONIMO STILTON and THEA STILTON names, characters, and related indicia are copyright, trademark, and exclusive license of Atlantyca S.p.A. All rights reserved. The moral right of the author has been asserted.

Based on an original idea by Elisabetta Dami.

www.geronimostilton.com

Published by Scholastic Inc., 557 Broadway, New York, NY 10012. SCHOLASTIC and associated logos are trademarks and/or registered trademarks of Scholastic Inc.

Stilton is the name of a famous English cheese. It is a registered trademark of the Stilton Cheese Makers' Association. For more information, go to www.stiltoncheese.com.

Text by Thea Stilton
Original title Mistero sull'Orient Express
Cover by Arianna Rea (pencils), Yoko Ippolitoni (inks), and Ketty Formaggio (color)
Illustrations by Sabrina Ariganello, Jacopo Brandi, Elisa Falcone, Michela Frare, Sonia Matrone, Federico Nardo, Roberta Pierpaoli, Arianna Rea, Arianna Robustelli, Maurizio Roggerone, and Roberta Tedeschi
Color by Cinzia Antonielli, Alessandra Bracaglia, Edwin Nori, and Elena Sanjust
Graphics by Paola Cantoni with Yuko Egusa

Special thanks to Beth Dunfey
Translated by Emily Clement
Interior design by Kay Petronio

12 11 10 9 8 7 6 5 4 3 2 1   12 13 14 15 16 17/0

Printed in the U.S.A.   40
First printing, November 2012

ALL BECAUSE
OF A STORM!

The **SUN** was setting over the Bosporus, streaking the sky with golden light. I was on the terrace of my hotel in Istanbul, Turkey. What a **fascinating** place! It was hard to believe that only a week earlier I had been in the middle of a **snowstorm**.

Yes, dear reader, I'd gotten **stuck** on a

ISTANBUL AND THE TOPKAPI PALACE MUSEUM

Istanbul is the largest city in the Republic of Turkey, and it's a very important historical, cultural, and commercial center. The Topkapi Palace Museum is located there. For about four centuries, the palace served as the primary residence of the Turkish sultans. In 1924, it was turned into a museum that houses ancient armor, classical antiquities, and other artifacts.

mountaintop during a CHALLENGING climb up Alaska's Mount McKinley.

Oh, pardon me. I almost forgot to introduce myself. My name is Thea Stilton, and I am a special correspondent for *The Rodent's Gazette*, the biggest newspaper on Mouse

Island. My brother, Geronimo, is the publisher.

Now, where was I? Oh, yes — a week before, I was **snug as a bug in a rug** in my comfortable, **stormproof** tent. I had a warm sleeping bag and plenty of cheese. But I was certain I would never arrive in *Paris* in time to catch my train!

You see, I had received a special invitation to travel on the most famouse train in the world, the Orient Express. The Paris police had found the legendary **Veil of Light**, an ancient wedding gown that had been stolen from the Topkapi Palace Museum in Istanbul nearly a century earlier.

Now, finally, the Veil of Light was headed back to Turkey on the Orient Express. But that storm made it impossible for me to get to France to join the gown's journey!

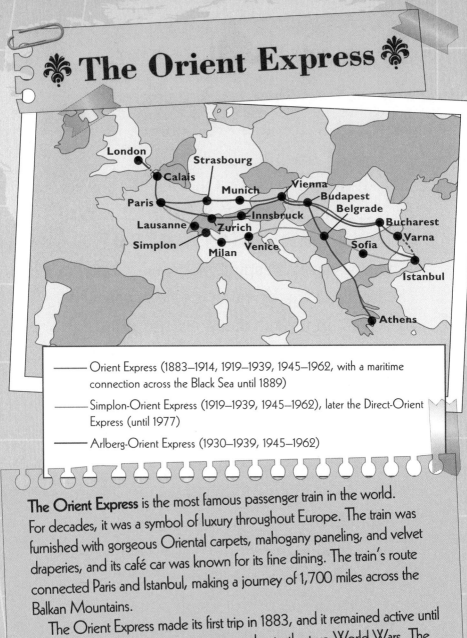

The Orient Express

Orient Express (1883–1914, 1919–1939, 1945–1962, with a maritime connection across the Black Sea until 1889)

Simplon-Orient Express (1919–1939, 1945–1962), later the Direct-Orient Express (until 1977)

Arlberg-Orient Express (1930–1939, 1945–1962)

The Orient Express is the most famous passenger train in the world. For decades, it was a symbol of luxury throughout Europe. The train was furnished with gorgeous Oriental carpets, mahogany paneling, and velvet draperies, and its café car was known for its fine dining. The train's route connected Paris and Istanbul, making a journey of 1,700 miles across the Balkan Mountains.

The Orient Express made its first trip in 1883, and it remained active until 1977, although there were interruptions due to the two World Wars. The most brilliant period in its history came between 1920 and 1930, when the train hosted royalty, artists, celebrities, and even international spies.

Initially, the train was known as the **Express d'Orient**, and it didn't go all the way to Istanbul; instead, passengers traveled to Varna and then took a ferry to Istanbul. By 1889, passengers could make the entire journey by rail. Over the years, the railroad company added new destinations and new tracks.

The Orient Express's prestige has lasted through time. Although the original route was discontinued in the 1970s, today there is a train known as the **Venice Simplon-Orient-Express** that connects London and Venice.

The Orient Express became well known thanks to novels by **Agatha Christie** and **Graham Greene**, who created homages to this special train.

That's when I had a brilliant idea. I needed someone to take my place on the train, and who better than the Thea Sisters? The THEA SISTERS are Colette, Nicky, Pamela, Paulina, and Violet — five **intelligent** mouselets I taught a while back in an adventure journalism class at my old school, **MOUSEFORD ACADEMY**.

I picked up my satellite telephone and placed a call to **MOUSEFORD**'s headmaster, Octavius de Mousus. It didn't take me long to persuade him.

"This is an educational opportunity the mouselets simply can't miss!" I told him.

"There will be lots of **celebrities** to interview. And the Thea Sisters' articles about the trip will be published in *The Rodent's Gazette*!"

THE ROARING TWENTIES

The news that the Thea Sisters would be taking an exclusive trip on the Orient Express threw Mouseford Academy into an **UPROAR**. Faster than you can squeak "pepperoni pizza with Parmesan on top," the mouselets were the center of attention. Their fellow students followed them around campus, **bombarding** them with questions.

Even Madame Ratyshnikov, the strict instructor of a NEW dance class, congratulated them on this *marvemouse* opportunity. She was thrilled that her students would be traveling on the same train as the great *ballerina* Zelda Mitoff!

As for *Colette*, PAMELA, *nicky*, **Violet**,

and PAULINA, they were excited and a little anxious. You see, they had very little time to prepare for their TRIP.

"We'll get to see Jack Nickmouse in the fur!" Nicky said.

"Who?" Paulina asked.

"The legendary golf champion," Nicky said. Her EYES sparkled with excitement. "And I might even squeak to him!"

Meanwhile, Violet, Pam, and Colette were collecting requests from friends who wanted an autograph from Raty Perry, the world's hottest POP STAR.

"The invitation says we're supposed to be in costume for the whole trip," said Paulina with **concern**. "We need to dress in the style of the 1920s. But there's no time to shop for the right clothes! We have to **leave** tomorrow."

Colette *smiled*. "Snout up, Paulina! I've got it all sewn up. Remember my friend Julie*? I called her last night, and she said she'd bring us an entire trunk of vintage clothing. She's going to transform us into five beauties from the Roaring Twenties!"

As soon as the mouselets heard Julie's name, they relaxed. Colette's pal was an up-and-coming clothing designer in Paris. She'd

---

* We met Julie in the book *Thea Stilton and the Mystery in Paris.*

definitely prevent them from committing any crimes of *fashion* in front of all those celebrities!

"The Roaring Twenties?" Pam said, giggling. "Do we have to dress like lions, tigers, and bears? **RRRRAAAAWR!** "

Violet laughed. "No, Pam! They're called the **ROARING TWENTIES** because back in the 1920s, World War One had just ended, and everyone was full of energy and **enthusiasm** . . . just like you!"

"Oooh, I'm so excited I could jump out of my **fur**!" Colette chirped. She began *TWIRLING* around the room.

Pam raised a **PAW** so her friends could slap her palm: "Give me five, sisters! This trip on the Orient Express is going to be absolutely fabumouse!"

The years between 1920 and 1930 are known as a period of great vitality and renewal. The world was recovering from the first World War, and fashion reflected the spirit of the decade. They were called "roaring" for the trust in progress and the determination with which people looked toward the future.

Clothing in this era was meant to be comfortable and give a sense of lightness and freedom. Thanks to new industrial processes, fashion became accessible to all, and new synthetic fabrics, like rayon, came to the forefront: They were soft, light, shiny, and even economical! Dresses with dropped waists, soft fabrics, and knee-length skirts (considered short at the time!) were the main elements of women's fashion in the 1920s. Women's makeup included lots of mascara and flaming-red lipstick. But the real sign of a woman in the Roaring Twenties was her haircut: The famous bob style was truly a revolution of the era, because up to this point only men had worn their hair cut short!

A TRIP THROUGH TIME

The next day, the Thea Sisters caught the **Ferry** to New Mouse City. Then they hopped on a direct flight to Paris.

The plane ride went by in a **BLUR**. Soon the mouselets found themselves at the Gare de l'Est, the oldest train station in Paris. That's where they were scheduled to board the Orient Express.

But when the mouselets arrived, the station was practically deserted. They were so early the conductor gave them a **FUNNY** look.

Luckily, a young porter with lively blue eyes came to their rescue. "I'm Claude, at your service. The train is still EMPTY," he explained. Then he winked. "So this is the perfect time to explore. FOLLOW ME!"

Claude moved confidently through the luxurious train. First he took the mouselets to the café car, where he served them cups of HOT cheese and croissants.

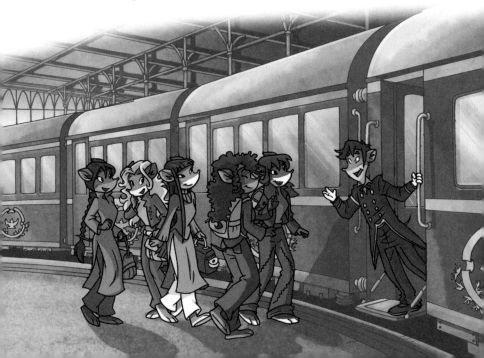

"It really feels like an old bistro from the 1920s!" Colette sighed, glancing at the piano and *small* tables that filled the café car.

Claude nodded. "That's exactly the feel we're going for! You see, the Orient Express is the only train that travels through time."

Once the mouselets had finished eating, Claude continued their tOUR. He led the Thea Sisters through a whirlwind of soft velvets, **precious** wood, French silverware, Bohemian crystal, and Flemish linen.

After they'd explored the length and width of the train, Claude stopped in front of a **CLOSED** door. Then he held his paw to his snout and looked around stealthily.

"This area is supposed to be off-limits, but for you I'll make an exception," he whispered *mysteriously*, taking a key out of his pocket. "This car was set up specifically as a showroom for the Veil of Light."

"SMOKIN' SWISS CHEESE!" Pam said loudly, making everyone jump.

"SSSSSSSSHHH, PAM!" the other mouselets shushed her. Claude stifled a giggle and invited his guests to enter.

It was dark, but Colette, Nicky, Pamela, Paulina, and Violet could make out a glass display case in the center of the train car. Inside the case, looking as though it were suspended in time, the Veil of Light shone brightly!

MALIK RATT III

The Thea Sisters stared at the gorgeous wedding gown. They were **wide-eyed** in wonder. Until . . .

"What are you doing here?!" thundered an unfamiliar **GRUMPY** squeak.

The mouselets all **JUMPED**. Behind them stood a *strange*, pudgy little rodent. His mustache, waistcoat, and elegant bow tie gave him the look of a gentlemouse from another **time**. He looked completely at home aboard the Orient Express. But the suspicious look on his snout did not bode well for the Thea Sisters.

Claude hurried to introduce the newcomer to the mouselets. "This is Chief Inspector Malik Ratt the Third, who is officially in charge of **protecting** the Veil of Light."

"You shouldn't be here!" the inspector squeaked sharply. "You'll have to *LEAVE* at once. Please don't get any closer to the display case!"

The mouselets quickly turned away. All except Nicky, who timidly stepped forward. "Excuse us, Inspector. We are students at **MOUSEFORD ACADEMY**, and we're here in place of Thea Stilton."

"I'm quite familiar with the **IDENTITY** of all the passengers," Ratt replied haughtily. He shot Claude a dirty look. "And none of them are allowed to be in here."

Embarrassed, Claude hurried the THEA SISTERS out of the compartment.

 Why did Inspector Ratt warn the Thea Sisters not to get too close to the Veil of Light?

"Inspector Ratt is famouse in his field," he explained. "He's the one who found the Veil of Light after years of SEARCHING. But he can't relax with the THREAT of the Cat Burglar hanging over his snout. . . ."

"The Cat Burglar?" Paulina repeated, intrigued. But there was no time to ask questions, because Claude had just thrown open three doors. "Here are your cabins! Two doubles and a single that CONNECT."

Then he scurried off, leaving the mouselets to admire their swanky rooms. Colette and Pam took the first cabin, while Nicky and Paulina chose the next one, and Violet took the single.

A moment later, Claude reappeared. "You have a visitor."

A mouse with short blonde fur was standing behind him.

"**Julie!**" the Thea Sisters exclaimed.
"**Mouselets!**" she greeted them, beaming.
Immediately, the cabin was filled with happy squeaking and the smack of kisses.

SMACK SMACK SMACK SMACK!

THE AMAZING JULIE

"Lucky you!" Julie exclaimed, looking around the cabin enviously. "A trip on board the Orient Express ... and in period costume! It's a fashionista's DREAM come true."

Claude pushed a large trunk into the cabin. Julie opened it solemnly. "And because this dream must be *très chic* ... voilà!"

The Thea Sisters gathered around the trunk. "Our clothes!" Colette exclaimed, clapping her paws in **excitement**.

The trunk was brimming over with clothes in the style of the 1920s.

"Hey, sister! Did you

rob Isaac Mousrahi's **showroom** or something?" Pam joked, TURNING OVER a veiled hat in her paws.

"Hee hee hee!" Julie giggled. "Colette didn't tell you? I work part-time at the Olympia Theater as an assistant costume designer. These are theater costumes, and my boss agreed to loan them to me. I had to promise they'd be well taken care of. But no worries — I TRUST you all completely."

In the twitch of a whisker, the Thea Sisters had transformed themselves from modern-day mouselets into roaring rodents from the 1920s. Colette, Nicky, Pam, Paulina, and Violet tried on one *lovely* outfit after another until each found the one best suited to her.

Violet wore a simple lilac shift with an

elegant belt around her hips. Pam put on a pair of **unusual** knee-length pants: They fit her like a glove! Paulina opted for an orange sailor dress with a pleated **skirt**. Nicky decided on a pair of pants and a jacket with a horseback-riding feel. As for Colette, she couldn't resist a light, swishy pink CHIFFON dress.

"Colette, that is simply *gorgeous* on you!" Julie said admiringly.

The rest of the mouselets agreed. "You've certainly found the perfect way to indulge your passion for fashion," Paulina noted.

Just then, they were interrupted by a noisy **DISTURBANCE** outside on the platform. Curious, the mouselets crowded around the window.

FiVE TRUNKS, OR SiX?

The Thea Sisters and Julie leaned out the cabin's windows to see what was going on. Soon they'd spotted the cause of all the **commotion**: The famouse guests had begun to arrive! A crowd of *enthusiastic* admirers had followed them.

"Look! It's **Jack Nickmouse** and Raty Perry, the ultimate power couple!" Julie squeaked with excitement.

A moment later, another rodent made her WAY triumphantly through the crowd, accompanied by thunderous applause.

"IT'S HER!" cried Violet, rushing out of the train. The other Thea Sisters looked at one another, bewildered. It was rare to see Violet so EXCITED, especially about a celebrity.

"Huh?" Pam said. "*Her* who?!" She and the rest of the mouselets scurried after Violet.

The moment they stepped on the platform, the mouselets were caught in an endless procession of **trunks** and hatboxes, which a team of porters was transporting on enormouse luggage carts. A **young** rodent with red fur was counting the bags by paw as they were loaded onto the train.

"Everything in order, Dimitri?" asked a **fluttering** voice, which made all the mouselets look in the same **DIRECTION**. That was the squeak of Zelda Mitoff! The famouse ballerina was TINY, but she scampered along in such a regal fashion that she seemed much taller than everyone around her. She was wearing a gorgeous green velvet wrap paired with a long, *ELEGANT* period gown.

"Five trunks and twelve hatboxes!" Dimitri responded immediately, bowing. "Nothing is missing, madame."

Zelda took the paw the young rodent

The other mouselets were distracted by Zelda Mitoff's arrival, but Paulina noticed that there were six trunks, not five! Is it possible that the famous ballerina's assistant miscounted?

offered her and stepped **onto** the train. She disappeared into a first-class car, leaving a trail of delicate PERFUME behind her.

"What an *elegant* rodent . . ." Violet sighed, entranced.

Paulina twirled her whiskers thoughtfully. "Yes, but what a **CHEESEBRAIN** that assistant is. There were six trunks, not five!"

"Zelda Mitoff walked right by and you were counting trunks?!" Violet **BLINKED** in disbelief. "Don't you know who she is? She's the greatest *ballerina* of all time! A *legend* of the dance world!"

"She's retired from the stage, right?" Colette asked CURIOUSLY.

"Yes," Violet confirmed. "She was already a prima ballerina when my mother was a mouselet. But she's still beautiful!"

"Did you see the **AMAZING** Jack

Nickmouse?" Nicky interrupted, her eyes **shining**. "I can't wait to interview him!"

"Looks like you better get in line, sister!" Pam said, **pointing** to a group of journalists getting onto the train. "We certainly won't be the only ones who want to squeak with the VIRs — Very Important Rodents. . . ."

Just then, there was a deafening whistle, and the conductor stepped onto the train. It was time to get back on board: The Orient Express was departing!

ALL ABOARD!

The Thea Sisters said good-bye to Julie, waving to her from the WINDOWS of the train.

"We'll keep you updated on everything, we promise!" Colette shouted as the train SLOWLY pulled away from the station.

No sooner had the train departed than it was time for the mouselets' first official business appointment: Inspector Ratt's PRESS conference.

The inspector waited until everyone had assembled. All of the journalists were HUNGRIER for news than a mouseling is for a cheesicle, and it was hard for them to keep quiet.

Finally, the inspector cleared his throat.

"We are returning the **Veil of Light** to its homeland," he squeaked sternly. "No one will be allowed to take it from Turkey again!"

"How do you know that the Cat Burglar won't succeed in STEALING it?" asked Priscilla Pawson, one of the journalists.

At the mention of the Cat Burglar, Paulina became *intrigued*. "Him again . . . ," she murmured.

Ratt smiled **enigmatically**. "I cannot reveal our secret methods to the public, ma'am. But I can guarantee you that the gown is safe. It is SECURED in an indestructible case, which not even I can open! Only the director of the Topkapi Palace Museum will be able to do so when I pass it *safely* into his paws."

"A highly publicized voyage on the Orient Express, and a *dangerous* thief on the loose . . . ," Nicky muttered to the others. "Inspector Ratt has a big job on his paws!"

Paulina nodded, pointing to the train's itinerary. "We'll cross six borders, with stops in Budapest, Sinaia, and Bucharest. At each stop, the gown will be shown to the public."

"It's sure to attract attention from all kinds of CRIMINALS!" Colette concluded.

Once the press conference had ended, the Thea Sisters and the other passengers returned to their cabins while the Orient Express sped along its course to Istanbul. The mouselets gathered in Colette and Pam's compartment to CHAT.

"All the reporters are waiting to see the Cat Burglar in action," Violet remarked.

"I noticed that, too, Vivi!" Paulina agreed. She switched on her laptop to look up more information about the Cat Burglar.

"Mouselets, Thea asked us to take her place on this trip. That means we can't let aɴything get past us!" Pam noted. "So let's review what we know while Paulina looks for news on this Rat Burglar. . . ."

"Not the Rat Burglar, Pam! It's the *Cat* Burglar!" Colette corrected her, laughing. "I did a little research before we LEFT, and I learned that the Veil of Light was a gift from the sultan Mustafa Shah to his favorite DAUGHTER, Siren. The gown was made

of silk, **woven** with pure gold thread, and studded with pearls and diamonds. It was so splendid and fine that it appeared to be woven of **light**! That's where its name comes from."

"Oh, here's something useful!" Paulina suddenly exclaimed. She'd been busy searching the **internet**. "Hmm, it seems that the Veil of Light has a rather **complicated** history. . . . ," she continued, clicking around. "It was one of the most **PRECIOUS** pieces in the Topkapi Palace Museum. On New Year's Eve 1922, the infamouse thief Rattamouche dropped down from a skylight and stole it!"

"Cheesecake!" exclaimed Pam. "And he pulled off the heist in spite of all the SECURITY in the museum?"

Paulina nodded. "**NO ONE** has ever

discovered how someone managed to pull off this job, especially because the **MUSEUM** was swarming with guards! The theft caused a huge **UPROAR**, and the name Rattamouche became famouse all over the world."

"So is he the Cat Burglar?" Violet asked.

"No, VIVI," Paulina replied. "But this is where the **story** gets really interesting! Listen to this. . . ."

A DOUBLE
CHALLENGE

The mouselets were hanging on Paulina's every word.

"See if you can guess the name of the inspector who devoted his whole life to CATCHING the thief Rattamouche and recovering the stolen gown," she continued in a MYSTERIOUS tone. "Just guess! That's right, it was none other than Malik Ratt!"

"What?" gasped Colette.

"Malik Ratt the First, that is!" Paulina explained. "He was the grandfather of the inspector who found the Veil of Light. The same inspector who is now traveling on this very **TRAIN** with us . . . right now—Malik Ratt III!"

"**Holey cheese!**" Nicky cried.

"That can't be a coincidence," Violet said.

"It sounds like the plot of a **movie**," Colette commented. "The grandson returns the precious artifact that was stolen from right under his own **grandfather's** snout!"

"He has not necessarily succeeded in returning it, though. . . . ," Paulina pointed out.

"This **Cat Burglar** must be very cunning, if even Inspector Ratt is nervous!" Pam observed.

Paulina tapped on her keyboard. "Oh, he's more cunning than a CAT, all right!" she said as she scrolled through another website. "And more agile. That's how he got his name. Most rodents believe the Cat Burglar is the

one who stole the *crown* right off the snout of the king of Belgium . . . during his **CORONATION** ceremony!"

"I heard about that!" Violet recalled. "The **Cat Burglar** is the same thief who stole the great violinist Yo-Yo Mouse's Stradivarius* — right in the middle of a **CONCERT**!"

"And he stole the hands off the face of Big Ben in London!" Paulina added.

"So he's an acrobat, and a **SPECIALIST** in impossible thefts!" Pam concluded.

Paulina nodded. "And now he's set his sights on the Veil of Light. **JUST WATCH!**"

---

* A Stradivarius is a violin made by the renowned craftsman Antonio Stradivari.

"'The Cat Burglar sent an open letter to all the major newspapers in Europe declaring a **challenge**,'" Nicky read over Paulina's shoulder. "'He wants to become more FAMOUSE than Rattamouche, and will prove his skill by stealing the Veil of Light from on board a moving train'!"

The mouseLetS drew closer to Paulina to read the letter.

"What if the Cat Burglar is already hidden on the train?" Violet wondered.

"*Sizzling spark plugs!*" Pam burst out. "Don't you realize, sisters? We're in the driver's seat on this one! The Cat Burglar could STRIKE at any moment!"

"Let's keep our eyes peeled," Paulina recommended. "It says here that the Cat Burglar is a master of disguise, so he could be any of the passengers."

Colette clutched her purse, straightened her hair, and grabbed the doorknob, ready to HEAD OUT.

"Well, let's get going, mouselets!" she exclaimed. "We have an entire **train** to search, dozens of rodents to meet, valuable information to learn, and, let's not forget . . ."

Her squeak trailed off.

Her friends **STARED** curiously at her. "Forget what, Colette?" Nicky asked at last.

"We've got gorgeous clothes to show off!" she finished with a **WINK**.

The Thea Sisters **burst** out laughing: Colette was truly hopeless!

TO CATCH A THIEF

The Thea Sisters decided to begin their search with the staff. They put their snouts together and divided up their assignments.

Pam slipped into the kitchen, where the world-renowned chef Charles Fromage was the undisputed *king* of appetizers and soufflés. As she **crept** between the steaming pots and pans, Pam couldn't resist sneaking a taste of a delicious batch of **cheese** puffs.

Colette got to know Roxanne, who worked in the boutique on the **train**. While chatting, the two mouselets discovered that they both collected tiny bottles of perfume. They became fast **fRieNDS** in no time!

Meanwhile, Paulina and Nicky did some **RECONNAISSANCE** in the café car. There they got to know Flora, a very lively

FROMAGE THE CHEF

ROXANNE THE SHOPKEEPER

Italian mouselet, and a real professional when it came to making mozzarella **SMOOTHIES**.

As for Violet, she was dying to get a closer look at the piano in the café's balcony. She walked up to the instrument *nervously*. She'd just sat down when Klaus, the pianist, **surprised** her by inviting her to play a duet!

FLORA
THE BARISTA

KLAUS THE PIANIST

The Thea Sisters met **FRIENDLY** rodents everywhere. The staff seemed ready to grant every wish and answer every **nosy** question — until the mouselets got to the last train car, where they came snout-to-snout with a **burly** mouse.

According to the name tag on his jacket, his name was Yusuf. He **EYED** the five mouselets suspiciously. "You can't go through

here!" he said **sternly**. "This car is for staff only."

The **mouselets** couldn't think of a way around him, so they had to retrace their steps.

"What a **mean mouse**," Pam spluttered with annoyance. "Who knew this train came with its own guard rodent!"

 Pam is right: Yusuf seems to be guarding something! But what?

A HOT MESS

That evening, the Thea Sisters sat down to an unforgettable first dinner aboard the Orient Express. Chef Fromage cooked his finest recipes, and the *elegance* of the passengers was worthy of the **red carpet** in Mouseywood!

The Thea Sisters settled into their seats and took advantage of the occasion to **observe** their fellow travelers.

In spite of — or perhaps because of — her **snooty**, standoffish manner, Zelda Mitoff was the most fascinating. Violet couldn't take her eyes off her. "She's truly a *grande dame!*"

Colette was more interested in **Jack Nickmouse** and *Katy Perry*. "How **ROMANTIC!** They seem so in love. . . ."

Meanwhile, the journalists were trying to worm their way CLOSER to the famouse guests. They were determined to get good quotes to put in their columns. They weren't on the hunt for the thief — they were on the hunt for a SCOOP!

After dinner, everyone moved on to the café car. Everyone, that is, except Zelda, who preferred to retire to her cabin. A few minutes later, her assistant, Dimitri, RETURNED to order a cup of hot tea for the ballerina.

Violet hesitated. She desperately wanted to interview Zelda, but she didn't have the **courage** to ask her assistant for an appointment.

Colette knew her friend well, and she could see that she was struggling. Unlike Violet, Colette didn't have a SHY bone in her body, so she didn't waste a second. She

scurried up to the bar to squeak with Dimitri when . . . **BAM!**

The two **COLLIDED**, and they both went flying. Madame Mitoff's cup fell and **shattered**. Boiling tea spilled all over Dimitri, soaking his shirt and **BURNING** the back of his right paw. Dimitri **frowned** and rubbed his paw, which was red and swollen.

Colette apologized immediately. "I'm so

sorry!" she cried. "Let's find a doctor for that."

"It's nothing," Dimitri said **hastily**. Then he hurried from the room.

The accident **ruined** the evening for poor Colette, who couldn't help feeling guilty. She certainly hadn't done it on purpose, but what a **cat-astrophe**! Not only had she injured an innocent rodent, but she'd also ruined Violet's chances of an interview with the famous ballerina.

"Well, that brings new meaning to the phrase '**HOT MESS**,'" she said with a sigh to Nicky when she returned to their table.

Nicky just laughed. "You get an *A* for effort, Colette! Don't get your tail in a twist. It was an **ACCIDENT**."

SO MANY
SUSPECTS . . .

The next morning, the Orient Express reached Budapest. The train stopped so its passengers could make a *quick* visit to the city.

The first to get off the train were Jack Nickmouse and Raty Perry. A **flaming-red** sports car was waiting for them at the station.

"**Crusty** carburetors, what a gorgeous **car**!" Pam sighed. She loved all **AUTOMOBILES**, especially race cars.

Raty and Jack didn't

seem to share her ENTHUSIASM. The singer whispered something to her companion. The expression on her snout was unreadable. She pointed to the train as if she wanted to go back on board, but Jack shook his snout nervously.

When Inspector Ratt glanced out his window, the two instantly fell silent. They got into the car and took off at full speed, DISAPPEARING from view.

The Thea Sisters exchanged looks: what strange behavior!

Violet waited a long time for Zelda to appear on the platform, but with no luck.

"Waiting for Zelda? Oh, my dear, you're as naive as a newborn mouseling," a voice sang out behind her.

It was Rhonda Ratwell, a well-known GOSSIP columnist. She stroked her

whiskers and continued, "The great Madame Mitoff hasn't let **anyone** get close to her since she retired from the stage."

"That's because she doesn't want anyone to see her wrinkles! **HA, HA, HA!**" snickered Priscilla Pawson, who had joined the little group.

Violet **blushed**. She was about to squeak up in defense of her favorite ballerina when an older journalist beat her to it.

"Don't mind those **BUSYMICE**!" he said, looking sideways at Rhonda and Priscilla. "Zelda isn't here because she never misses her **MORNING** workout, no matter where she is. Why, she's in such great

shape, she could return to the stage tonight if she chose to."

"So why doesn't she?" Violet asked eagerly. "It would be **amazing** to see her dance!"

The journalist sighed with regret. "Zelda would still be a great *ballerina*, but she

would just be a **shadow** of the Zelda of long ago! She can't help comparing herself to what she used to be."

Violet and the journalist chatted during the trip to Budapest. The mouselet was very *surprised* to learn that she was squeaking with none other than Eliot Albamouse, the **eminent** critic from the *Mouseford Courier*.

PABLO AND PEGGY

At dusk, the Thea Sisters returned to the **train** and discovered that two more VIRs had joined the party. They were the wealthy HEIRESS Peggy Rattfeller and the Spanish painter Pablo Picamouse.

They were a truly strange-looking couple: She was quite large, and he was quite SKINNY. But these were the least of the differences between them.

Peggy was very shy and seemed to shun

the spotlight, which was exactly the opposite of the arrogant, **ornery** Pablo! The two were rumored to be just friends, but many suspected that their **feelings** ran deeper . . . or at least that was what the Orient Express's gossip columnists, Rhonda Ratwell and Priscilla Pawson, believed.

The Thea Sisters found the famous **PAINTER** squeaking heatedly with the police inspector. "My painting is a **MasteRPiece**! It must arrive at the Topkapi Palace Museum without a scratch," Pablo **BARKED**. "I *demand* to know what kind of security measures you are using!"

"On the Orient Express, there is a very secure safe," Ratt replied in a tone that was **COOLER** than cottage cheese. "Why don't you paw your painting over to the conductor?

He'll take care of you. There's no reason to worry."

"A simple safe won't be enough to stop the Cat Burglar!" Pablo scoffed. "I know all about his **THREAT** to steal the Veil of Light!"

"That won't happen," Chief Inspector Ratt replied, his expression darkening. "If the **Cat Burglar** dares climb on board this train, he'll be getting off in pawcuffs!"

The Thea Sisters weren't the only ones to witness this angry EXCHANGE between the painter and the police inspector. A small CROWD of journalists and staff had gathered to watch the fireworks.

Colette noticed Dimitri and quickly checked to see how his right paw was faring. The burn was very bright. Colette's ears drooped with embarrassment. She felt GUILTIER than a gopher in a gerbil burrow.

Meanwhile, the conductor had intervened in the discussion between Inspector Ratt and the famouse painter. "Come with me. I'll show you our safe," he suggested to Pablo. "You'll see that it's very secure. Your painting will not be at risk, I promise!"

A SQUEAK in THE NiGHT

The train sped through the night, rushing through the Romanian **mountains**.

The Thea Sisters were exhausted from their busy day. They climbed into bed and fell asleep as soon as their snouts hit their pillows.

A little past midnight, they heard a shout in the corridor.

"YOU CHEDDARFACE!"

The Thea Sisters **LEAPED** up. They immediately recognized the screech of Pablo Picamouse.

"What was that?" Pam asked.

The mouselets peeked out into the corridor. The painter was right outside their door, and he was extremely **anGRY** at Dimitri. The **YOUNG** rodent seemed to be apologizing for something, but Pablo's **SHOUTS** drowned out his squeaks of protest.

The doors to other cabins had opened, and the passengers were trying to shush the furious **PAINTER**.

"What's all the fuss about? We're trying to sleep!" Rhonda protested.

"This rude rodent pushed me!" Pablo shrieked.

"I asked your pardon," Dimitri murmured unhappily.

"Oh, *now* you apologize?" the painter cried. "That's not what you said before. It was more like 'Get out of my way, shortytail!'"

Suddenly, a scream much sharper than Picamouse's rang out.

"EEEEEEEEEEEEEEEEK!"

"What's going on?" Pablo cried. "Who's making all that racket?"

Colette rolled her **EYES**.

Rhonda pointed to the next compartment. "The **SCREAM** came from in there!"

"But that's where the **Veil of Light** is

being kept!" Priscilla said.

Everyone scurried to look, but in their hurry they tripped over one another's tails. When they finally managed to enter the compartment, it was completely DARK. A steward was sitting on the floor with a **bump** on his head!

"What happened?" asked Eliot Albamouse.

"Are you hurt?" Paulina asked, kneeling down to help the POOR aching steward.

The steward didn't answer. He just pointed at the OPEN door to the exhibition room.

The Thea Sisters **peeked** inside. Even in the dim light, they could see the display case. It was shut, but . . .

EMPTY!

The crystal display case was *empty*! How could the thief steal the Veil of Light without breaking the case?

THE EMPTY CASE!

The passengers stood in the doorway, frozen with shock and **FEAR**. No one dared enter the compartment until Inspector Ratt arrived. He immediately took charge of the situation, turning on a **flashlight** and shining it around.

There was someone lying on the ground. It was Peggy, and she had fainted!

"**Peggy**, my little Brie lump, what happened to you?" Pablo Picamouse cried.

The inspector motioned to him not to get closer. "She needs air!" he explained, gently slapping the **heiress's** snout to revive her.

Peggy opened her eyes and looked around in confusion. "The thief! He's here!"

"Don't worry, the thief has gone," the

inspector reassured her. "But tell me, did you get a good look at him?"

Peggy **GLUMLY** shook her snout.

Eliot and Pablo helped Peggy get **UP**. Meanwhile, the inspector was gazing at the EMPTY display case. "Tell me what happened," he said to Peggy.

She took a deep breath. "I . . . I was coming back here to get my fan. I had forgotten it! When I came in, it was completely dark, so I looked for a light switch, and then —"

"What did you see *exactly*?" the inspector pressed her.

Peggy gulped. "I saw a **THIEF** all dressed in black. He was meddling with the display case. I **SCREAMED**, and then I must've fainted!"

"I'm sure it was your scream that made him run away, madam," the inspector declared.

"The **Cat Burglar**!" Pablo exclaimed.

"He stole the Veil of Light!" Rhonda and Priscilla said at the same time.

"**Calm down**," the inspector said. "There's no need to be alarmed. Nothing has been stolen."

Everyone **STARED** at him, their snouts hanging open in surprise. They looked like a pack of hungry cats whose food had run away.

PLAN B

Violet was the first to regain her squeak. "What do you mean, the thief hasn't **STOLEN** anything, Inspector?" she asked. "The case is empty!"

Chief Inspector Ratt placed his paw on the glass case and nodded. "It's *always* been EMPTY. This exhibit is just a holographic image."

"H-holo-what?!" Peggy stuttered, **confused**.

But Paulina understood immediately. "What a clever way to protect the Veil of Light!" she cried. "Holographic images are very sophisticated projections that appear to be real objects." She approached the case and peered in. "Inside the base there's probably a hidden laser projector that

HOLOGRAMS

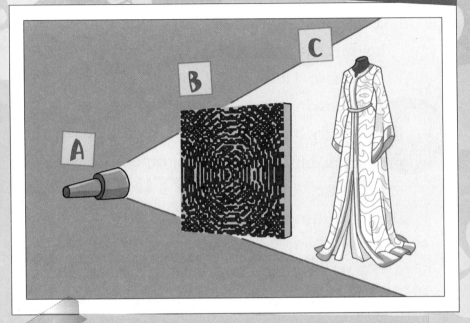

Thanks to hologram technology, it's possible to create a photographic image that gives the impression of depth without using a lens.

Using a laser beam (A), a special plate on which an image of the object has been imprinted (B) is illuminated. As the light passes through the plate, it projects a three-dimensional image (C). Observers can even walk around and look at the back of the image, as if it were a real object!

makes it look like the *gown* is really there."

The inspector **LOOKED** at Paulina in surprise and then smiled. "Exactly.

Knowing that the Cat Burglar would try to steal the Veil, I decided to trick him with a holographic image. That way, I could **CAPTURE** him without putting the real gown at risk. But it seems that my plan has failed!" he said *worriedly*. "And now the thief knows that the Veil of Light was never in this compartment."

The Veil of Light must be in the last train car! thought Colette. *Under the watch of the charming Yusuf!* She shot her friends a look. They all had the same idea.

Meanwhile, it was late, and everyone was tired. Most of the passengers **RETURNED**

The Veil of Light isn't really in the exhibition room — Inspector Ratt's plan has protected it from the attempted theft. So where is the real Veil?

to their compartments without asking any more questions.

The Thea Sisters were the last to leave the exhibition room. Violet managed to catch a whispered **EXCHANGE** between the conductor and Inspector Ratt.

"Now what do we do, Inspector?" the conductor asked, worried.

Ratt looked at him and declared, "It's obvious. We go to **PLAN B**...."

CHANGE OF PLANS

The next morning, the train **ASCENDED** the towering mountains that surround Sinaia, Romania.

After the tumultuous events of the previous night, no one wanted to have **breakfast** in their own cabin. No one except for Zelda Mitoff, that is. Everyone else gathered in the restaurant car. They were eager to learn the latest news about the **iNVESTiGATiON**.

Dimitri was among the first to arrive, and Colette noticed with relief that the burn on the back of the assistant's paw had healed. Actually, it seemed to have completely disappeared!

The mouselet was about to ask him how it

The burn on the back of Dimitri's paw has disappeared very quickly. But how?

had healed so *QUICKLY*, but Paulina held her back, pointing to something outside the window. "Look how beautiful it is!"

Not too far in the distance they spotted the ENCHANTING Peleş Castle.

The train conductor entered the restaurant car. "There has been a *change* of plans," he announced. "We're having TROUBLE with the air-conditioning, and it will take a

TRANSYLVANIA

In the heart of **Romania** lies the region of **Transylvania**. The Carpathian Mountains create an extraordinarily beautiful landscape, with many snow-covered peaks, tree-covered plateaus, and mysterious caves at the base of the mountains. The **Transylvanian Plateau** extends into the middle of this ancient mountain range.

Transylvania is famous for its castles, some of which belonged to Vlad III, whom many believe to be the basis for the legendary fictional character Count Dracula.

Bran Castle is often associated with Vlad III. But it is not known for certain whether Vlad III ever lived there.

Peleş Castle is one of the most beautiful castles in Romania. It rises up out of the woods, surrounded by mountains.

The castle was built by **King Carol I**, the first king of Romania. Construction began in 1873, and the castle was finally completed in 1914. It functioned as the royal residence from then until 1947.

Today the castle serves as a museum that holds paintings, tapestries, drawings, sculptures, and fine furniture. Peleş Castle has **160 rooms**, which still contain their original furnishings.

few hours to repair it. To avoid unnecessary discomfort to our passengers, we're **extending** the visit to Peleş Castle. You will dine there and spend the night in the castle."

The passengers **exchanged** puzzled looks as the conductor continued. "Our staff has organized a twenties-style **ball** for the occasion!"

The Thea Sisters were delighted about the change of plans, but the conductor's story didn't **convince** them.

"I can't help being suspicious about this **BREAKDOWN**," Violet commented as they returned to their cabins. "I'll bet the inspector doesn't want the passengers on board while he puts '**PLAN B**' into action!"

Pamela **NODDED**. "I agree. But what do you think **PLAN B** could be?"

"I'm sure we'll find out tonight," Colette

said. "In the meantime, I'm so excited! I've always **dreamed** of going to a ball in a real castle. Plus, it'll be a great opportunity to **OBSERVE** the other passengers up close. . . ."

Colette headed straight for Julie's trunk. "Let's choose our most glamorous dresses, **mouselets**! Tonight's going to be special, I can feel it!"

DINNER FIT FOR A KING!

That afternoon, the mouselets and their fellow passengers boarded elegant carriages for the trip to **Peleş Castle**. Violet and Paulina climbed into a carriage with Colette and Pamela, while Rhonda and Priscilla fought to win the only seat left next to *Raty*

Perry. They were hoping to **extract** a few good **QUOTES** during the journey. Unfortunately, Jack Nickmouse wasn't traveling with Raty, and that made the singer crankier than a wet cat in a rainstorm. She didn't utter a **SINGLE** word during the trip.

So just where was Jack Nickmouse? He was with Nicky! They had both decided to ride up to the castle on **horseback**. The air was **BRISK**, and both were eager for a good ride.

Jack **launched** his horse into a gallop, and only Nicky's talent as a rider allowed her to keep up.

"I love the **peacefulness** of golf," Jack said when he finally stopped to let his horse rest. "But I couldn't live without a bit of adventure! The **thrill** of the unexpected, the risk of the unknown . . . these are the things I crave most when I travel."

Hmm, thought Nicky. *Jack is the most athletic rodent aboard the Orient Express. And he's constantly traveling, often to the most exotic and exclusive places. If he is the thief, he certainly wouldn't pass up this chance for adventure!*

But a second later, she **shook** her suspicion from her snout. "I agree, Jack! That is, I mean, um, Mr. Nickmouse!"

The golfer burst into a deep laugh and invited her to call him by his first name.

The pair took off at a trot, *chatting*. So Nicky got much more than an interview: It turned into a long conversation between **FRIENDS**.

When they reached the castle, they found Raty Perry waiting for Jack in the GARDEN. By now, she was grouchier than a rodent with a trap on her tail.

"Come on, Jack, MOVE those paws!" she urged him. "We're going to be late!"

Nicky was surprised by the singer's grumpy tone. Was Raty Perry JEALOUS of her? That seemed absurd! Perhaps she was AFRAID that the golf champion had revealed too much. . . .

Something smells funnier than feta cheese, Nicky thought.

Then she scurried off to FRESHEN up and change her clothes: Dinner would be served soon.

In the luxurious dining room, the chef and the staff from the Orient Express had created a BANQUET fit for kings. The mood at the table was so cheerful that Zelda even started to squeak to Violet, who was seated next to her. When the famous ballerina discovered that the mouselet was the daughter of Chen Lu, a great orchestra conductor, the ballerina promised to give her an exclusive interview!

At the end of the dinner, the atmosphere was so relaxed and jolly that everyone decided to start dancing right away.

LET'S HOOF IT!

The orchestra broke into a **lively** Charleston, a popular dance from the Roaring Twenties.

As soon as she heard the music, Colette exclaimed, "Let's hoof it, mouselets!" She **winked** at her friends, who were looking at her quizzically. "That's how they used to say 'let's dance' back in the 1920s," she explained.

The Thea Sisters were among the first on the dance floor. They couldn't wait to kick up their paws.

"We're **LUCKY**, mouselets," Paulina observed. "This party came at just the right moment! Let's check out the guests and try to figure out who could be the **Cat Burglar**."

"Don't forget, the thief could also be one of the staff," Pam said.

"Oh, don't worry, I haven't," Paulina replied. "But the staff have a lot of work to do, and not very much free time on their paws. The **thief** needs to be able to do whatever he'd like whenever he'd like."

"Be **ALERT**, sisters!" said Colette.

The five young **investigators** mixed with the dancers, ready to snatch any useful details in between steps.

Pablo Picamouse and Raty Perry launched into a **WILD** fox-trot: They were perfect partners! To Pamela, it seemed like these two were **old** friends.

Just friends? What if they're accomplices? the mouselet thought. *They've both been to the fashionable places where the Cat Burglar has struck most often. . . .*

While Pablo **danced**, poor Peggy was

left on her own. The wealthy heiress was dressed in an outfit that wasn't very flattering, and she was covered in flashy, **mismatched** jewelry.

"I don't like to be catty, but I've never seen someone with so little **TASTE** in clothing!" Colette WHiSPeReD to Paulina.

"You're **RiGHt**, Colette," her friend agreed. "Her **pearls** almost seem fake."

Colette nodded. "I'm going in for a closer look!" She danced **close** to the heiress and then returned to her friend's side. "It's true — they're **FAKER** than fat-free cheese!"

"**FAKE?!**" Paulina replied. "But she's supposed to be a millionaire! How **WEIRD** . . ."

Colette glanced over at Peggy again. "Are we sure that she's *really* a **millionaire**? What if it's all an act to **deflect** suspicion?"

"I just can't see Peggy as the Cat Burglar," Paulina replied.

"Her, *non*, but Pablo, *oui!*" Colette said. "He's so full of himself! Playing the part of the thief would make him feel **important**. And they could be working together. Think back to last night. Maybe Pablo distracted the inspector and the other passengers by making that **scene** with Dimitri while Peggy went into the compartment to steal the **precious** gown!"

"But that can't be. After all, she was the

one who sounded the **ALARM**!" Paulina objected.

"What are you two plotting?" Claude interrupted. "Don't tell me you're already out of *breath*!"

Without waiting for a response, he took Colette and Paulina by the paws and PULLED them out to the middle of the floor to dance the *Charleston*!

THE SUSPECT
SHUFFLE

Colette was busy ***dancing*** when she found herself facing Dimitri. Her gaze fell on the ratlet's **paw**. Suddenly, she **STUMBLED**.

"Time for a break," Paulina suggested, offering her a ***cool*** drink. "You're really letting your fur down tonight."

Colette took her friend aside. "Look at

Dimitri's paw," she whispered. "His burn is back!"

Paulina smiled. "Relax, Colette, I'm sure he knows you didn't do it on purpose."

Colette shook her snout. "No, you don't understand. This morning the BURN was gone! I was so happy that it had healed, but now it's back. Isn't that strange?"

Paulina STARED at Dimitri. He realized he was being watched, and smiled.

"Oops! He saw us!" CRIED Colette.

Paulina tried to act natural. She HOPPED back onto the dance floor. Colette followed her reluctantly, murmuring, "If the burn was healed this morning, how could it be there now . . . ?"

But soon, the rhythm of the music won her

The burn on the back of Dimitri's paw has reappeared! How could the same paw be healed in the morning and injured again in the evening?

over, and she forgot all about Dimitri and his burned paw. "Shake those tails, mouselets!" she called to her friends.

The **PARTY** continued late into the night, and Zelda Mitoff didn't sit down for a single dance. It was as if she were a **young mouseLet** again! Violet watched her with admiration — until a strange suspicion crossed her mind. *Staying in such good shape would make it easy to do all kinds of acrobatics*, she thought. *What if Zelda is the Cat Burglar?*

Violet was **shaken** by the thought that the great ballerina could be involved in something so **SHADY** — until she recalled one of her grandpa Chen's favorite sayings: "In the dark, all rats are black." Now she could see the wisdom of his words: Without clear proof, anyone could appear **GUILTY**!

Late that night, the mouselets returned to
the large bedroom where they'd be sleeping
during their stay in the **CASTLE**.

"The Cat Burglar could strike at any
moment, and we still have so **far** to go!"
Violet commented.

"Yeah," Paulina agreed. "The thief could
be anyone, and for all we know, he or she
could have a **HENCHMOUSE**! Let's review
our suspects."

There's Peggy, the heiress who wears fake pearls. What if she's actually broke? One big score as the Cat Burglar could make her rich again!

There's Pablo, the painter, a conceited rodent who loves to be the center of attention. Stealing the Veil of Light would make him feel like the star of the show!

There's Zelda, the legendary ballet dancer. She trains every day and keeps to her cabin ... but why?

The Cat Burglar could be any one of the passengers. Who do you think is the thief?

There's Jack, the golf star. He loves danger and adventure, just like the Cat Burglar!

There's Raty, the pop star. She and Jack are the ultimate power couple. But is that just in romance, or also in crime?

There's Dimitri, Zelda's assistant. One minute his paw looks burned, and the next it's healed. But how?

"Whew! Seems like everyone's a suspect!" Pam joked. She fell back onto the bed, **exhausted**.

"Can't we rule out Dimitri and Pablo Picamouse?" Paulina asked. "Those two were in the corridor *arguing* during the attempted robbery."

"But what if their argument was part of the plan?" Nicky objected.

Colette SiGHeD as she removed the shoes from her aching paws. "OOF! I'm too tired to think, mouselets."

"You're right, Colette," Violet agreed. "What we need now is a good night's sleep. Let's continue our **investigation** tomorrow!"

THE MISSING
PAINTING

The next day, the passengers all **returned** to the train, and the mouselings headed straight for the café car. As soon as they'd boarded, the conductor announced that they would **SKIP** their planned stop in Bucharest to make up the time they had lost.

The Thea Sisters decided to review what they knew about their **traveling** companions over breakfast. They were more determined than ever to discover the **identity** of the Cat Burglar.

As Dimitri passed by their table, Colette shot a **worried**

look at his paw. It was still red and swollen.

I must have been dreaming yesterday morning, she thought. She was both annoyed and reassured to see the *familiar* burn on Zelda's assistant's paw. *I was so sure that it was healed!*

At that moment, the conductor **BURST** into the café car with some **disturbing** news: "Mr. Picamouse's painting has been stolen!"

"**WHAT???**" Pablo thundered. He

turned pale as a slice of mozzarella. Then he staggered and fell into Peggy's paws.

A moment later, he had recovered. He **LEAPED UP** and scurried out of the compartment. Almost everyone followed him. The journalists didn't want to miss this chance to hear what the HOT-BLOODED painter would squeak next!

The passengers HURRIED down the corridor of the train and jammed into the conductor's office. The safe was wide open, but not a single piece of jewelry had been taken. Only the painting was missing!

"I told you not to let it out of your sight!" Pablo BARKED. "This thief knows the value of great works of art."

Chief Inspector Ratt was as GREEN as mold on aged cheddar. This theft was truly a BLOW!

"I was so focused on the Veil of Light that the thief took the opportunity to break into the SAFE," he muttered to himself.

"Well, the PAINTING must still be

on board the train," Violet guessed. "So there's a good chance we can find it."

Inspector Ratt stared at her, surprised that someone had heard him. "What did you say, **MISS**?"

"When we got back on the train this morning, the painting was in its place," Violet observed. "Otherwise the CONDUCTOR would have noticed it was missing when he placed the **jewelry** in the safe.

The train hasn't **stopped** since then, so . . ."

"So the thief is STILL on board, and the PAINTING is with him!" Pam concluded.

"Right!" the inspector said. "No one could get off the *moving* train without setting off the security alarm on the doors."

"There's a sophisticated security system on the Orient Express?" Paulina marveled.

"This train is *faithful* to the original in almost every single way," Inspector Ratt explained. "But it does have **modern** security systems built in."

The inspector invited everyone to gather in the café car. Each passenger would have to account for his or her whereabouts from the time the train **departed** until the discovery of the theft. If the PAINTING was still on board, Inspector Ratt would find it!

"I feel like we're living in an Agatha Christie novel," Violet murmured. "He wants to collect our alibis!"

PEGGY'S ALIBI

Inspector Ratt spent the next half hour meeting with each passenger, collecting testimonies. As soon as he'd finished, he cleared his throat. "It seems," he began **SERIOUSLY**, "that at the moment of the theft, everyone was seen in a place **faR** from the safe. Everyone, that is, except . . ."

Everyone held his or her breath. All **EYES** were on the chief inspector. It was so quiet you could hear a cheese slice drop.

After a moment of suspense, the inspector declared, ". . . except you, Miss Rattfeller!"

Everyone turned and looked in disbelief at the heiress, who seemed to **SHRINK** into her fur. Peggy stuttered, "I—I stayed in my cabin to rest. When I left for a moment, I

SMACKED into Mr. Dimitri! I stepped on his paw, right, Mr. Dimitri?"

"That is **RIDICULOUS**!" Zelda cried. "My assistant was with me the entire time! I was **dictating** my autobiography."

Peggy's whiskers trembled. The heiress **mumbled** for a moment and then fell silent.

Pablo Picamouse's painting is missing, but whoever stole it didn't hide it very well. In fact, it can be found in the very train car where all the passengers are assembled! Can you spot it?

Hint: Look in the window, behind Pam and Violet!

"Miss Rattfeller," Inspector Ratt said, "your **aLiBi** doesn't hold up. I must **search** your cabin! Please come with me."

Peggy nodded and followed him.

"I can't believe it! Peggy Rattfeller, a thief?" Pam said in DISBELIEF.

"Yeah! I can't imagine her sneaking into the conductor's office and **breaking** into the safe," Nicky agreed.

"I'm with you, Nicky," Violet said. "It just doesn't make sense! She said that she **BUMPED** into Dimitri outside her cabin. But he was with Zelda, and he couldn't have been in TWO places at the same time!"

Nicky nodded. **"THAT'S RIGHT!** Although . . ."

"Although . . . ?" asked Colette, who still felt a bit **nervous** whenever Dimitri's name came up.

"He was late this morning, remember?" Nicky continued. "I was going to the café car when I passed Dimitri going in the *opposite* direction. He was in a big hurry, with his necktie undone and his fur all ruffled — and he was **limping**!"

"As if someone had **STEPPED** on his paw . . . ," Paulina said slowly.

"That's **right**!" Nicky nodded **seriously**. "And there's more: I reached the café a moment later, and in came Dimitri, looking **perfectly** put together. He was wearing a different

suit and walking **normally**!"

"But his cabin is far from the café car," Violet protested. "How could he change so *QUICKLY*?"

"Now that I think of it," Pam **interrupted**, "I noticed something **STRANGE**, too! At the castle, Dimitri turned **DOWN** Chef Fromage's dessert. He said he's ALLERGIC to chocolate. But during the first dinner here on the **train**, I saw him drink a big chocolate shake!"

"What about the burn on his paw?" exclaimed Colette. "Today it was **bright red** again, but yesterday . . ." Her squeak trailed off. "Nicky, when you ran into him, did you notice if it was red or not?"

Nicky **squinted**, trying to remember, then responded confidently. "His paw was completely healed!"

The mouselets fell ⬛SILENT⬛. They were deep in thought.

WHAT DO YOU THINK?

How could Dimitri be in two different places at the same time? Let's review the clues:

- On the day the Orient Express departed, Dimitri counted five trunks in Zelda's luggage, but there were actually six.

- The young assistant's paw was burned by a cup of boiling tea ... but the burn on his paw keeps disappearing and then reappearing!

- Peggy Rattfeller said she saw Dimitri just before the painting was stolen, but Madame Zelda claims that he was in her cabin the whole time.

- Dimitri acts very strangely: One moment he says he's allergic to chocolate, then later he eats it. One moment his clothes are disheveled, and a few minutes later he's put together and wearing a completely different outfit!

THE SIXTH TRUNK

The Thea Sisters were stunned into squeaklessness. What a **strange** set of clues!

"There's only one explanation for a paw that's **RED** one moment and not the next," Colette concluded solemnly. "There are two right paws, and therefore two Dimitris!"

"Two Dimitris?" Pam asked. "Do you mean . . . identical twins?"

Colette nodded. "Maybe! Or at least two rodents who look similar enough that they appear to be the same mouse, as long as they're seen **SeParaTelY**!"

Paulina **smacked** a paw against her forehead, surprised that she hadn't thought of it sooner. "Of course!" she exclaimed. "So

If there are two Dimitris on the train, that explains everything! One twin was with Zelda, transcribing her memoir, while the other ran into Peggy and Nicky.

Peggy stepped on one twin's paw while the other Dimitri was with Zelda, scribbling down her memoir!"

Nicky still wasn't completely convinced. "But the NIGHT the thief tried to steal the Veil of Light, Dimitri was ARGUING with Pablo in the corridor—"

"He did that on purpose!" Pam interrupted. "Remember what Pablo Picamouse said? He

While Pablo was busy with Dimitri in the corridor, Dimitri's twin tried to steal the Veil of Light!

said that it was Dimitri who started the **argument**! At the time, we didn't believe him because he kept SCREAMING his snout off. But Pablo was telling the truth: It was actually Dimitri who started the squabble. He was trying to DISTRACT everyone while his twin stole the Veil of Light!"

"It all fits!" Paulina agreed. "It also helps explain the other robberies by the Cat Burglar: No one has ever been able to catch him because they were looking for just one thief, when actually there were two. That's how Dimitri and his twin have been able to create the perfect alibi and throw the **INVESTIGATORS** off their trail."

The Thea Sisters spent a few moments reflecting on this *incredible* discovery. Each mouselet thought through the details. Had the **mystery** really been solved?

"There's still one problem," Colette said at last. "How did the other Dimitri get on board the Orient Express without being seen? Where has he been hiding all this time?"

There was a long pause while the mouselets thought it over.

"The trunks!" Paulina suddenly exclaimed, making the others **JUMP**.

"The trunks?" Violet asked.

Paulina nodded. "Zelda had six trunks loaded onto the train, not five like Dimitri

said. I'm **sure** of it, I counted them myself! And I'll bet that the sixth **trunk** is in Dimitri's cabin. That's where he's hiding his twin!"

A GAME OF CHESS

All the pieces of the puzzle were coming together. But Violet raised one last question. "Only one of the twins went to **Peleş Castle**. The other must have stayed on the *train* so he wouldn't be discovered. But there's something I don't understand. He had the whole night to open the safe and steal the painting, but instead he **waited** until everyone was back on the train to do it!"

"Mumbling mufflers!" Pamela exclaimed. "That really is strange!"

"It can't just be by chance," Paulina observed. "The Cat Burglar doesn't leave anything to chance."

Violet nodded. "It's like a game of chess. There's a reason behind each move."

Violet's words created a powerful image in

the **mouselets'** heads: the Cat Burglar and **INSPECTOR RATT** locked in an intense chess match!

Nicky, Colette, Paulina, and Pam all *turned* to Violet — she was the Thea Sisters' resident chess expert. But she was too busy **_thinking_** through different moves for kings, queens, rooks, and pawns to notice their anxious glances.

Suddenly, she **lit up**: "Of course! It's a surprise attack!"

The other mouselets looked at her in **confusion**.

"What do you mean by 'surprise attack'?" Paulina asked.

"You move a piece, pretending to **threaten** your opponent, but you're really opening the way for another of your more **DANGEROUS** pieces," Violet explained. "Your opponent focuses on the immediate damage and doesn't realize that you've begun a fatal attack on another front!"

"So if I'm following your train of thought," Colette squeaked slowly, "the Cat Burglar has stolen the **PAINTING** to distract Chief Inspector Ratt."

"That's right," Violet agreed. "If he forces the inspector to investigate a less important theft, then he's free to **ATTACK** the Veil of Light!"

"Easier than stealing cheese chunks from a mouseling," Nicky said, shaking her snout. Then she sprang to her paws. "Well, what are we waiting for? Let's go WARN the inspector! There's not a minute to waste."

"Just a moment," Colette said. "We still think the Veil of Light is being kept in the last train car, right? So wouldn't it be better if two of us kept an EYE on that car while the others go find the inspector?"

Everyone agreed. So the mouselets separated. Nicky, Paulina, and Pamela ran to alert Inspector Ratt, while Colette and Violet SCURRIED toward the last car. They were ready for a SHOWDOWN with the unstoppable thief!

A SHADOW ON THE ROOF

As Nicky scampered down the deserted corridor, she was DISTRACTED by the view outside the window. The Orient Express was crossing the Danube River valley, passing over flat countryside. But **suddenly**, something on the ground below caught her eye.

The SHADOW of the moving train was visible on the ground next to the tracks. But there was something else there. . . .

"Mouselets, LOOK!" Nicky shouted. "He's up there!" She had spotted the shadow of someone scurrying across the train's roof!

"It's him! The Cat Burglar!" Pamela exclaimed.

Paulina agreed. "Who else could scale the roof of a *moving* train?"

"He must be going after the **Veil of Light**!" Nicky cried. "We have to find out how he got up there."

Within a moment or two, the three mouselets had discovered a WINDOW in the ceiling that allowed access to the roof. A ROPE kept it partly ajar.

Nicky turned to Pam. "Give me a paw, and I'll follow him **up** there!"

"No, Nic!" Paulina warned her. "It's too DANGEROUS!"

"I know, but this is an emergency. We can't let the Cat Burglar escape! Besides, I'm in **better shape** than the mouse who ran up the clock. I can do it! I'll hold on **TIGHT** to the rope the thief used. You go get the inspector

while I follow him onto the roof."

"I'm coming with you! It's **SAFER** if we're both up there," Pam declared. She put out her paws, ready to boost Nicky up.

"I'll go get Inspector Ratt!" Paulina agreed. "But wait for us before you do anything. . . ."

Nicky had already scrambled up, and Paulina boosted Pam up after her. There was no time to waste!

A CHEESE-CURDLING CHASE!

Nicky and Pam tried to move very carefully. They were **TERRIFIED**, but they knew they had to act quickly or the thief would escape with the *precious* Veil of Light.

When Pam popped her head outside the trapdoor, the strong **WIND** created by the fast-moving train knocked her **FLAT**. For a moment, the **mouseLet** thought she would be blown away like a balloon!

But Nicky was right next to her, ready to catch her. "Hold on to the ROPE and stay low!" she shouted.

Between the *hiss* of the wind and the clanking of the train, the noise was deafening, making it difficult to communicate. The two mouselets stayed **CLOSE** together as they tried to get their balance. It took them a few minutes, but finally they both managed to *MOVE* forward.

Nicky took the first step, and then the second. Soon she was able to move at a steady Pace. She proceeded cautiously, one paw after the other, toward the back of the train. She didn't dare raise her snout for fear that she'd lose her **balance**, but moving like this, she could hardly see her whiskers in front of her nose!

Pamela followed her step by step. She was so **LOW** to the ground she was practically CRAWLING.

Eventually, Nicky stopped to catch her breath and take a look around. She and Pam hadn't been able to **catch** the thief: The roof of the train in front of them was EMPTY.

"Oh no, he's escaped!" Nicky whispered. She was sure that the thief had already dropped down into the last car. At that very moment, he probably had his **dirty paws** on the Veil of Light! Or maybe he was outside the last compartment, going snout-to-snout with Yusuf.

But Nicky was certain of one thing: The **Cat Burglar** had no idea that they were onto him. *The element of surprise is our only advantage*, she thought. And she figured that Violet and Colette would probably already be inside the compartment with Yusuf.

So she screwed up her COURAGE and continued moving forward, in spite of the **train's** jerks and jolts. A few minutes later, she and Pam had struggled all the way to the last car.

no WAY in!

While Paulina rushed to find the inspector, and Nicky and Pamela tried to **REACH** the last car from above, Colette and Violet made their way to the door of the last train car. As usual, Yusuf was guarding the entrance, completely BARRING the door.

The two mouselets begged him:

"OPEN THE DOOR!"

"Please! The thief is inside!"

Yusuf glared at them, scowling. "**NO ONE GETS IN!** This car is reserved for the staff. I've told you this before, mouseLets! How many times am I going to have to repeat myself?"

Colette tried to be patient. "It's very

important, Mr. Yusuf! The thief is stealing the **Veil of Light** right now, we're sure of it!" she explained **calmly**.

"No one is allowed through here!" the guard replied **STUBBORNLY**.

So Violet stepped forward and brought out her secret weapon: one of **Grandpa Chen's** proverbs (although actually she had just

invented it at that very moment!). "My grandpa always says, 'Those who wish to be good **GUARDS** must not lose sight of the object they are watching'!"

Yusuf didn't **MOVE** a whisker.

"That means that you need to go inside to see if the gown is still in its place!" Colette cried impatiently. "While you're standing here guarding the door, the **Cat Burglar** has probably come in through the window or something," she added.

Little did Colette know that her **PREDICTION** was coming true at that very moment!

Yusuf lowered his eyes to look at the *frantic* snouts of these two strange mouselets. Violet and Colette had a moment of hope: Were some doubts SCRATCHING through the guard's tough **ARMOR**?

But it was not to be. "Orders are orders!" Yusuf replied, staring off into EMPTY space again.

The two mouselets sighed in frustration. There was nothing they could do!

A HiGH-TECH TRiCK

While Violet and Colette were pleading with the **UNMOVABLE** Yusuf, Nicky and Pamela had reached the roof of the *last* train car.

"Oh, my goodmouse!" Nicky cried. "Look at this, Pam! The thief *cut* an enormouse **HOLE** in the roof!"

Pam crawled over to her. "The thief did this?!" she exclaimed.

"Yeah . . . ," Nicky said, still hardly able to believe her **EYES**. "Like a hungry cat opening a tin of sardines! But how?"

The answer was right in front of them. A few feet away lay a red box with a small tube sticking out of it. The box's **label** read **LIQUID NITROGEN**.

Nicky and Pam scrambled over to examine the box. "It's a portable GENERATOR with liquid nitrogen for a laser cutter," Nicky exclaimed. "I didn't think these came in such small sizes."

"**WOW!**" Pamela said. "These things cut through slabs of metal like a knife through cream cheese. This thief is more than just an acrobat — he's also super TECH SAVVY!"

The two mouselets leaned over carefully to peek inside the hole. Below them, a mouse in a black bodysuit was **WORKING** close to a case that held the Veil of Light. A dark hood **covered** his snout.

"It could be Dimitri or another young, athletic rodent," Nicky squeaked quietly.

If the thief had raised his **EYES**, he would have seen Nicky and Pamela watching him from above. But he was focused on his task: attaching a harness to the glass case.

Suddenly, he noticed the **reflections** of the two mouselets on the panes of glass in front of him. The thief almost **JUMPED**, but then he **STOPPED**

himself. He didn't want Nicky and Pamela to know that he had noticed them. He didn't have time to worry about two nosy mouselets!

oNE DOWN!

Meanwhile, Paulina had scurried along the entire length of the Orient Express in search of Inspector Ratt. He wasn't in Peggy's cabin. She asked everyone she saw, but no one could **HELP** her — until she ran into . . . Dimitri, the Thea Sisters' number one **suspect**!

Paulina stopped and looked at his paw. It was still **ReD**!

Dimitri asked her politely, "Is everything all right, miss? You seem upset."

Paulina tried to think *quickly*: The twin with the burned paw was just steps from her, while his brother was in the middle of stealing the **Veil of Light**! She had to do something. But what?

"I'm looking for Inspector Ratt," she responded, a bit **HESITANTLY**. "It's urgent!"

Dimitri looked her up and down. "I heard he went back to the **safe**. Maybe I could give you a paw?" he said in an amused squeak.

Paulina grabbed his paw, pretending to be more **tired** than she really was. She couldn't let him slip away!

"Actually, I'm a bit out of breath. . . . ," she panted. "And I can't quite remember the way to the safe. Would you be so **KIND** as to accompany me?" she asked.

"Uh, okay . . . ," said Dimitri.

Together, the pair headed toward the **safe**, where they found the inspector and the train conductor.

By this point, Paulina had regained her courage. She **PUSHED** Dimitri into the

compartment in front of her.

Inspector Ratt looked shocked at her strange behavior. "We saw the **Cat Burglar** running on top of the train, toward the last car!" Paulina explained. "Nicky and Pam are *chasing* him! Please, you have to come with me! But first, arrest Dimitri: He's the Cat Burglar's **ACCOMPLICE**!"

TOO LATE!

Nicky and Pamela were starting to get worried: Why hadn't Violet and Colette **burst** into the **TRAIN CAR** yet? They couldn't believe that Yusuf wouldn't let their friends in. After all, this was an **EMERGENCY**. There was hardly any time to keep the thief from *escaping*!

"But how will he get away without being discovered?" Pam asked.

"That harness must be for transporting the case with the **Veil of Light**, but how does he think he's going to get it out of there?" Nicky wondered.

"Maybe Dimitri and his twin have a **henchmouse** arriving by **helicopter**," Pam guessed, looking far off into the sky.

Nicky **shook** her snout. "I don't think so . . . but there's no time to find out. There's no one here to arrest him. We're going to have to **STOP** him ourselves!"

And so they did. **HOLDING** on to the rope that the Cat Burglar had used before them, the two mouselets dropped into the train compartment.

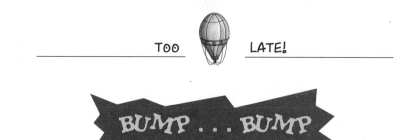

BUMP ... BUMP

When the Cat Burglar saw them dive in from the roof, an amused *grin* spread across his snout.

"**Ha Ha Ha!** You're too late, my little cheese niblets," he said.

Pam and Nicky exchanged a quick look: They needed to delay the **THIEF** if they had any hope of preventing him from escaping.

"You won't be able to get the case out of here," Pamela said, **POINTING** to the harness. "That thing is **HEAVIER** than the world's biggest block of petrified Parmesan!"

"**Ha Ha Ha!**" the thief laughed again. "You think I'm going to try to carry it out on my back? You must take me for a real cheesebrain!"

THE CAT BURGLAR'S PLAN

1 A hot-air balloon that fits through the hole in the ceiling . . .

2 . . . a superstrong harness tied around the case holding the precious gown . . .

3 . . . and the Cat Burglar, ready to disappear into thin air!

That's it, keep on squeaking! Tell us how brilliant you are! Nicky was thinking. *The others will be here any second now with Yusuf and the inspector, and then we'll see if you're still laughing!*

The thief pointed to the straps of the harness. "**нa нa нa!** In another minute, I'll press this button, a hot-air balloon will blow up, and the **Veil of Light** and the **Cat Burglar** will soar into the sky! **нa нa нaaa!**"

Nicky and Pam glanced at each other in despair. It looked like the Cat Burglar was going to get away with it again!

But suddenly . . .

BAMMM!

The door flew open and a deep voice echoed through the compartment:

"Paws up!"

THE HOAX

Yusuf *loomed* in the compartment door, which suddenly seemed much smaller. Nicky and Pam could just barely make out Violet and Colette standing behind the GUARD. But the Cat Burglar didn't seem the least bit **intimidated**.

"Time's up, my little cheese puffs!" he said,

laughing. He grabbed the harness straps. As soon as the hot-air balloon was inflated, he would FLY out of the train with the precious gown!

But what happened next didn't **exactly** go as the Cat Burglar had planned. . . .

Suddenly, the Veil of Light disappeared from inside the crystal case. In its place stood a stern rodent with **THICK** gray whiskers!

"What in the name of cheddar is *that*?" the scoundrel muttered, spinning around to gaze with **HORROR** at the case and its contents. He was so stunned he let go of the **STRAPS**.

"H-how . . . W-what . . . ? I . . . I don't understand!" spluttered the **ASTOUNDED** thief.

Nicky and Pam took advantage of his confusion. They *threw* themselves at

the Cat Burglar. Nicky grabbed him by the tail while Pamela **KNOCKED** him off his paws with a tackle worthy of the National Mouseball League.

But . . .

SWISH . . . SWISH

. . . the thief wriggled out of their grasp like a **slimy sewer rat**! His bodysuit was covered in a slippery substance that made it impossible to get a grip on him.

That was when Yusuf, Violet, and Colette came to the **RESCUE**. They had just realized what the thief had planned to do with his strange **tools**.

Yusuf launched himself across the compartment at the **Cat Burglar**. At the same time, Violet and Colette pulled the train's manual brake.

Screeeeeeeeeeeeech!

The Orient Express shook, jerked violently, and stopped *SUDDENLY*. A moment later, Paulina and Chief Inspector Ratt hurried into the compartment.

The inspector had a strange **SMILE** on his snout. In his paws, he held a small object that looked like a remote control.

Everyone looked around for the Cat

Burglar. In all the commotion, they'd lost sight of him. Where had he gone?

Pamela raised her eyes to the ceiling. All she saw was BLUE sky. There was no sign of the hot-air balloon.

"Did he escape?" she asked, confused. "Did anyone see what happened?"

No one answered. Then they heard a moan.

Pamela saw a paw in a black glove waving from beneath Yusuf's enormouse bulk. She burst out laughing. "Ha Ha Ha! Even the most slippery customers are no match for Yusuf!"

The stern guard gave no response, but the barest hint of a smile flitted across his snout.

TWO THIEVES in ONE!

Inspector Ratt pawcuffed the Cat Burglar immediately to make sure that he wouldn't WRIGGLE away when Yusuf got up.

The Thea Sisters hugged one another. Colette, Paulina, and Violet were **happy** and relieved that Nicky and Pam had survived their adventure on the train's roof!

"AHEM!" the inspector COUGHED to get their attention. "I think you mouselets deserve the honor of revealing the thief's identity." He pointed to the hood that was still covering the SCOUNDREL'S snout.

Nicky, Pamela, Paulina, and Violet pushed Colette forward. "Go on, Colette!" Pam said. "If it wasn't for the **scalding** you accidentally gave him, we never would have figured it out."

The mouselet timidly approached the Cat Burglar. With a quick, *deft* move, she removed the hood from his snout. Under a mass of messy **fur**, the thief's eyes shone with fury.

Colette *smiled* and said politely, "My name is Colette, what's yours?"

"Leon!" the thief **grumbled** reluctantly. His snout was completely identical to his twin's! "Dimitri and I would have gotten away with it if it weren't for you meddling mouselets!"

Now there was just one **mystery** left to solve: Who was the rodent inside the case?

"It's another projection," the inspector explained, **winking** slyly. "It's Malik Ratt the First, my grandfather!"

The inspector looked as happy as a **MOUSELING** on Christmas morning. "You see, I made a SMALL adjustment to my original plan B. I wanted the thief to believe that the Veil of Light was kept in the last train car, guarded by Yusuf. We used the same **TRICK** here as in the **EXHIBITION** car — a projection of the gown."

"So where is the real gown, then?!" Colette asked, bewildered.

Everyone turned anxiously to look at the inspector. He laughed. "It's already in **Istanbul**. The two fake cases were designed to contain identical holographic images, perfect reproductions of the gown and my **GRANDFATHER**. I used this remote control to switch the projections."

Chief Inspector Ratt pushed a **button**. The image of his grandfather disappeared, and the wedding gown reappeared.

"Wow, it seems so **real**!" Pam said, pressing her snout against the glass.

Ratt *pushed* the button again, and the image of his grandfather reappeared.

"See how easy it is?" he exclaimed. "My grandfather dedicated his whole life to finding the **Veil of Light**. It seemed right that he be present in some way when the Cat Burglar was **CAPTURED**."

PARTY AT THE TOPKAPI PALACE MUSEUM!

When the Orient Express reached the station in Istanbul, word of the Cat Burglar's capture had already circulated on the **internet**. Inspector Ratt was welcomed as a hero, and a day of celebration was declared in his honor. He brought the THEA SISTERS with him and thanked them for their *invaluable* help.

Together, they drove down Istiklal Caddesi, the main street in Istanbul. The sidewalks were teeming with rodents cheering them.

All the passengers from the Orient Express participated in the CELEBRATION, and even Peggy got a moment of glory: She

was the one who found Picamouse's **missing** painting! The heiress had ordered a cup of hot cheese in the café car, where she noticed the lost painting sticking out from its hiding place. Her discovery came as an enormouse relief to her dear friend Pablo!

At the end of the day, the guests assembled at the Topkapi Palace Museum and waited **EAGERLY** to see the Veil of Light. But minutes kept slipping by without anything happening.

The journalists were beginning to gossip

about the possibility that the precious gown had been stolen again when suddenly the lights went out and a **beam** of light illuminated the *grand* terrace outside.

Everyone scurried out, and their snouts dropped open in **surprise**. While sweet, sad music filled the air, the magnificent Zelda Mitoff began to **DANCE**. She

was wearing the **Veil of Light**!

Violet was moved to tears.

"In light of the extraordinary situation, Zelda agreed to dance one last time," explained Eliot Albamouse.

"She's hoping everyone will forget that the **Cat Burglar** was her own assistant!" hissed Priscilla Pawson.

"Not exactly," Paulina corrected her. "Dimitri was a substitute for the real assistant, who mysteriously quit a few days before the Orient Express was due to ***depart***."

But it was the kind theater critic who had the last word. "Actually, what really convinced Zelda was the enthusiasm of a young detective who wanted to see her perform!"

Violet **blushed** from snout to tail. Her friends put their paws around her, delighted to see her so *happy*.

But no one was as delighted as I was when I met the mouselets at the museum and they told me all about their journey. As always, the Thea Sisters proved the power of teamwork and had a truly **THRILLING** adventure!

THEY WERE MORE THAN FRIENDS. THEY WERE SISTERS!

Thea Sisters

Don't miss any of my other fabumouse adventures!

Thea Stilton and the
Dragon's Code

Thea Stilton and the
Mountain of Fire

Thea Stilton and the
Ghost of the Shipwreck

Thea Stilton and the
Secret City

Thea Stilton and the
Mystery in Paris

Thea Stilton and the
Cherry Blossom Adventure

Thea Stilton and the
Star Castaways

Thea Stilton: Big Trouble
in the Big Apple

Thea Stilton and the
Ice Treasure

Thea Stilton and the
Secret of the Old Castle

Thea Stilton and the
Blue Scarab Hunt

Thea Stilton and the
Prince's Emerald

Be sure to read these stories, too!

#1 Lost Treasure of the Emerald Eye

#2 The Curse of the Cheese Pyramid

#3 Cat and Mouse in a Haunted House

#4 I'm Too Fond of My Fur!

#5 Four Mice Deep in the Jungle

#6 Paws Off, Cheddarface!

#7 Red Pizzas for a Blue Count

#8 Attack of the Bandit Cats

#9 A Fabumouse Vacation for Geronimo

#10 All Because of a Cup of Coffee

#11 It's Halloween, You 'Fraidy Mouse!

#12 Merry Christmas, Geronimo!

#13 The Phantom of the Subway

#14 The Temple of the Ruby of Fire

#15 The Mona Mousa Code

#16 A Cheese-Colored Camper

#17 Watch Your Whiskers, Stilton!

#18 Shipwreck on the Pirate Islands

#19 My Name Is Stilton, Geronimo Stilton

#20 Surf's Up, Geronimo!

#21 The Wild, Wild West

#22 The Secret of Cacklefur Castle

A Christmas Tale

#23 Valentine's Day Disaster

#24 Field Trip to Niagara Falls

#25 The Search for Sunken Treasure

#26 The Mummy with No Name

#27 The Christmas Toy Factory

#28 Wedding Crasher

#29 Down and Out Down Under

#30 The Mouse Island Marathon

#31 The Mysterious Cheese Thief

Christmas Catastrophe

#32 Valley of the Giant Skeletons

#33 Geronimo and the Gold Medal Mystery

#34 Geronimo Stilton, Secret Agent

#35 A Very Merry Christmas

#36 Geronimo's Valentine

#37 The Race Across America

#38 A Fabumouse School Adventure

#39 Singing Sensation

#40 The Karate Mouse

#41 Mighty Mount Kilimanjaro

#42 The Peculiar Pumpkin Thief

#43 I'm Not a Supermouse!

#44 The Giant Diamond Robbery

#45 Save the White Whale!

#46 The Haunted Castle

#47 Run for the Hills, Geronimo!

#48 The Mystery in Venice

#49 The Way of the Samurai

#50 This Hotel Is Haunted!

#51 The Enormouse Pearl Heist

And coming soon!

#52 Mouse in Space!

Meet
GERONIMO STILTONOOT

He is a cavemouse — Geronimo Stilton's ancient ancestor! He runs the stone newspaper in the prehistoric village of Old Mouse City. From dealing with dinosaurs to dodging meteorites, his life in the Stone Age is full of adventure!

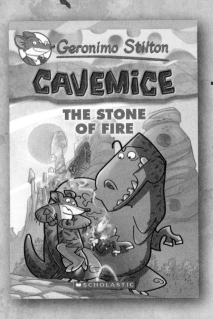

THE STONE OF FIRE

The Stone of Fire — the most precious artifact in the Old Mouse City mouseum — has been stolen! It's up to Geronimo Stiltonoot and his cavemouse friend Hercule Poirat to retrieve the stone from Tiger Khan and his band of fearsome felines.

Don't miss these very special editions!

THE KINGDOM OF FANTASY

THE QUEST FOR PARADISE:
THE RETURN TO THE KINGDOM OF FANTASY

THE AMAZING VOYAGE:
THE THIRD ADVENTURE IN THE KINGDOM OF FANTASY

THE DRAGON PROPHECY:
THE FOURTH ADVENTURE IN THE KINGDOM OF FANTASY

THEA STILTON:
THE JOURNEY TO ATLANTIS

Thea Stilton's first hardcover!

Meet
CREEPELLA VON CACKLEFUR

I, *Geronimo Stilton*, have a lot of mouse friends, but none as **spooky** as my friend CREEPELLA VON CACKLEFUR! She is an enchanting and MYSTERIOUS mouse with a pet bat named Bitewing. YIKES! I'm a real 'fraidy mouse, but even I think CREEPELLA and her family are AWFULLY fascinating. I can't wait for you to read all about CREEPELLA in these fa-mouse-ly funny and **spectacularly spooky** tales!

#1 THE THIRTEEN GHOSTS

#2 MEET ME IN HORRORWOOD

#3 GHOST PIRATE TREASURE

#4 RETURN OF THE VAMPIRE

THANKS FOR READING, AND GOOD-BYE UNTIL OUR NEXT ADVENTURE!

TheaSisters